Jayden is the leader of the Samurai Power Rangers. As the Red Ranger, it is his job to protect our world from danger.

Jayden's father was a Power Ranger, too. He defeated the evil Master Xandred and trapped him in the Netherworld.

Mentor Ji trained Jayden to become a master Samurai. Now that Jayden's training is complete, he is ready to become the leader of the Samurai Power Rangers.

"But I'm used to fighting alone," Jayden told Mentor Ji. "I don't want to put anyone else in danger."

"More and more of Xandred's henchmen, the Nighlok, are coming into our world to do evil. I think Xandred may be very close to breaking out from the Netherworld," said Mentor Ji.

Mentor Ji knew that Jayden needed help.

"There are four others who have trained for these dark days," Mentor Ji added. "They await the call to join you and fight as Samurai Rangers."

Suddenly, the Gap Sensor was activated. That meant a powerful Nighlok had entered our world.

"Jayden, we cannot wait any longer. The time has come to summon your team of Samurai Rangers," said Mentor Ji.

"Are you sure I'm ready to lead?" Jayden asked his mentor.

"One Samurai is strong. But a team is unbeatable," Mentor Ji told him. "Just remember your father's words as he left for his final battle."

Jayden remembered what his father told him: "One day the great responsibility of being the Red Ranger will fall to you," he had said. "Remember, protect the world from evil, stand by your allies, and never run from a battle."

"You're right, Ji," Jayden said. Just like his father, it was his destiny to protect our world from Master Xandred. "I will never forget my father's last words. I must not fail. I am the Red Ranger."

"The other Rangers have spent their whole lives preparing to fulfill their Samurai destinies," said Mentor Ji. Then he fired four magic arrows into the air. "Fulfill your destiny to lead them."

Each of the four arrows found the other Power Rangers—Kevin, Mia, Mike, and Emily. This was the call they had trained all of their lives for. They knew that it was their destiny to join with the Red Ranger and protect our world.

Kevin is the Blue Ranger. He was a champion swimmer before joining the Samurai Power Rangers.

Kevin is able to harness the power of Water into his Spin Sword, which morphs into the mighty Hydro Bow. His Zord is the Dragon.

The Pink Ranger is Mia. She is confident and sensitive, and acts as the big sister of the group. Mia gets her powers from the Air. Her Spin Sword morphs into the Sky Fan. Her Zord is the Turtle.

The Green Ranger is Mike. He is the free spirit of the team and enjoys skateboarding and video games.

Mike's element is the green Forest. His Spin Sword morphs into the Forest Spear. His Zord is the Bear.

The Yellow Ranger, Emily, is the youngest of the team. She grew up in the country and had never been to the city until she joined the Power Rangers.

She is the master of the Earth element. Her Spin Sword morphs into the Earth Slicer. Her Zord is the Ape.

Jayden, Kevin, Mia, Mike, and Emily introduced themselves—this was the first time the five Samurai Power Rangers stood together.

But there wasn't much time for getting to know one another. They had a Nighlok to fight!

The Power Rangers charged off to battle the
Nighlok. Tooya and an army of Moogers had
snuck into our world and were putting humans
in danger. It would take a team of Samurai
Rangers to stop them.

The Rangers looked down at Tooya and his army of Moogers.

"Who are you guys?" Tooya asked.

"We're the Samurai Rangers!" Jayden replied proudly.

The Rangers activated their Samuraizers.
This is the device that morphs them into
Samurai Power Rangers.

"Go, go, Samurai!" all five Rangers shouted. Then they each drew their special Kanji symbols in the air. This is what begins the Morphing Sequence and activates Samurai Ranger Mode.

The Rangers began the Morphing Sequence
into Samurai Rangers. Together they called out,
"Rangers together, Samurai forever."

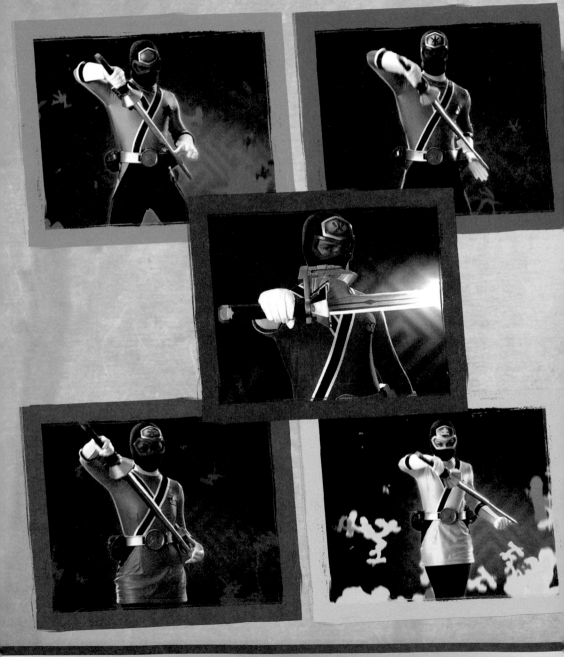

Once they had morphed, the Red Ranger led
the Samurai Power Rangers into battle.
"Moogers, get them!" Tooya commanded.

"I'm going to fillet all you fish faces," the Blue Ranger yelled to the Moogers as he swung his Spin Sword.

But the Moogers surrounded the Power Rangers.

"There are dozens of them," the Yellow Ranger said.

"They just keep coming," added the Pink Ranger.

"We can do this," the Red Ranger said to the others. "Samurai Rangers are always stronger when they work together."

As the Moogers closed in, the Green Ranger said, "I've got more than one trick up my sleeve." He placed the Bear Disc on his Spin Sword. This transformed his sword into the Forest Spear.

"Spin-cycle Sayonara!" the Green Ranger yelled as he swung his powerful spear and took out a team of Moogers.

Then the Red Ranger upgraded his Spin Sword to the Fire Smasher.

"I'm thinking this will make an impact on you," the Red Ranger said as he struck down Tooya.

But it takes more than that to defeat a Nighlok!
Each Nighlok has two lives. Its second life is as a
giant MegaMonster that towers over the city.
To battle these MegaMonsters, the Rangers
need to call upon their own Mega Mode.

To engage Mega Mode, each Ranger uses his or her Samuraizer to write the Kanji symbol for *large* over their FoldingZord. This begins the Zord's morphing sequence into a gigantic Zord vehicle.

When the Rangers fight together in Mega Mode they can defeat any MegaMonster!

Tooya blasted the Rangers as they charged forward.

"Time to wipe that smile right off your skirt!" shouted the Yellow Ranger.

Then each Ranger attacked Tooya from a different side.

But it was the Red Ranger's final strike that knocked out that nasty Nighlok.

"Samurai Rangers, victory is ours," the Red Ranger called out as the Nighlok exploded.

"We could have never done it without each other," Jayden said to the other Power Rangers. They looked at each other and knew that it was true: Rangers together, Samurai forever!